For Dawn  J.O.

To Lindsey and Rabbit from the girls x  L.G.

# OXFORD
UNIVERSITY PRESS

Great Clarendon Street, Oxford OX2 6DP

Oxford University Press is a department of the University of Oxford.
It furthers the University's objective of excellence in research, scholarship,
and education by publishing worldwide in

Oxford  New York

Auckland  Bangkok  Buenos Aires  Cape Town  Chennai
Dar es Salaam  Delhi  Hong Kong  Istanbul  Karachi  Kolkata
Kuala Lumpur  Madrid  Melbourne  Mexico City  Mumbai  Nairobi
São Paulo  Shanghai  Taipei  Tokyo  Toronto

Oxford is a registered trade mark of Oxford University Press
in the UK and in certain other countries

Text © Jan Ormerod 2005
Illustrations © Lindsey Gardiner 2005

The moral rights of the author and illustrator have been asserted

Database right Oxford University Press (maker)

This Bookstart edition first published 2006

British Library Cataloguing in Publication Data available

ISBN 978-0-19-279207-5  (Bookstart paperback)
ISBN 978-0-19-271988-1  (Paperback and audio CD)

7  9  10  8

Printed in China

Paper used in the production of this book is a natural,
recyclable product made from wood grown in sustainable forests.
The manufacturing process conforms to the environmental
regulations of the country of origin

# Doing the Animal BOP

## Jan Ormerod and Lindsey Gardiner

OXFORD
UNIVERSITY PRESS

IF you like to **dance** and you sometimes **sing**,

why don't
you do the
animal thing?

put your heels together,

and **Waddle** along.

High stepping knees
and feathers that

bounce-

flim-flam
flutter

to the **ostrich** flounce.

jive and jiggle –

just don't stop!

Jump and wiggle

to the monkey bop.

**Kick** those legs like the **donkeys** do.

Then go hee-haw hee-haw, too!

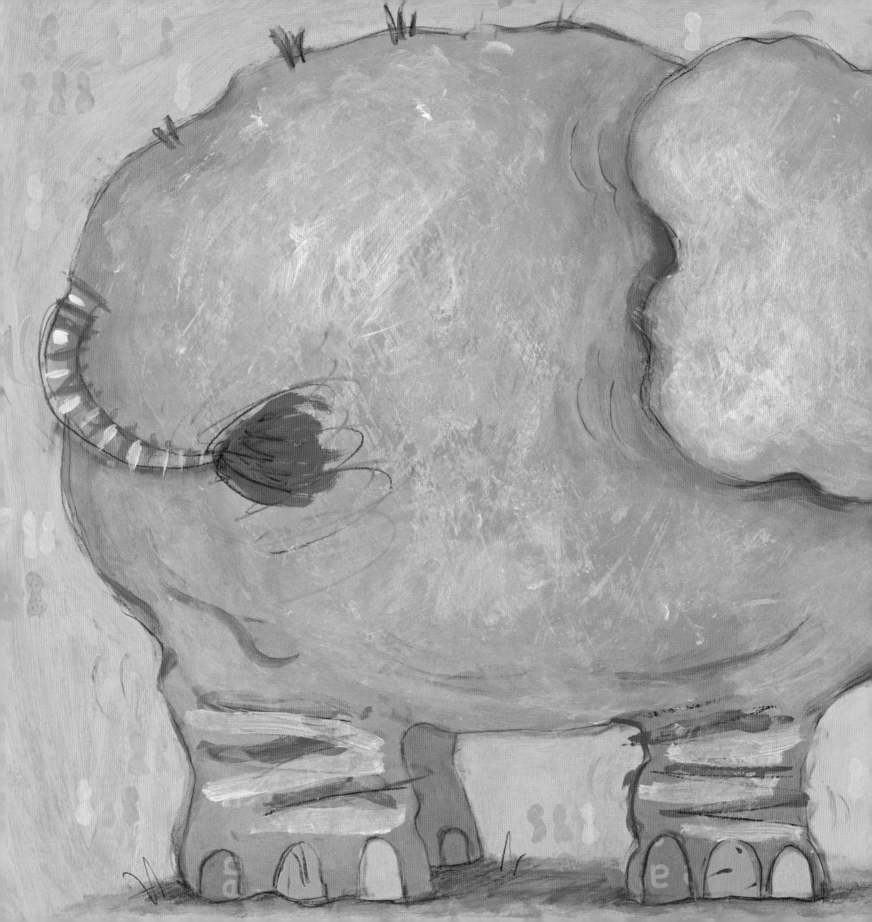

Wave one ARM.

STOMP your feet.

Trudge along to the elephant beat.

Move **one** leg.

Now move **two** . . . . . . . move the way that the **lizards** do.

... and a chicken can **CLUCK**.

But I think it's more fun being a **duck** ...

The duck does a **waddle**

on his **fLIP-flAP** feet,

Roar and rage,

it's a rhino romp!

All the **COW** can do is chew.

So let's end up with a great big

mmmmoooooooooooooooooooooo

moooooooooooooo

°oooooooo